The Chocolate Candy Kid

Sheila Lavelle

Illustrated by

Glenys Ambrus

A Belitha Press Book

MARILYN MALIN BOOKS
in association with ANDRE DEUTSCH

Chapter 1

The bar of chocolate had been lying in Kathy's pocket all afternoon like a secret treasure. All through Miss Potter's boring old nature lesson Kathy had thought about nothing else. Now that school was over she could enjoy it at last.

She peeled off the paper wrapper and bit into the layers of candy and chocolate and caramel. It had cost most of her pocket money, but it was worth every penny. Cooper's Candy Bars were the best chocolate bars in the world.

Kathy licked the last traces from her fingers and sighed. No more Cooper's Candy Bars until pocket-money day came round again. She was dropping the paper sadly into the bin outside the school gate when somebody grabbed her arm.

'Hey, don't throw that away, our Kath,' a voice said. 'It's worth money.' And the chocolate wrapper was rudely snatched from Kathy's hand.

Kathy scowled. She hated her cousin Ginger with all her heart. Even more than she hated spiders, and spinach, and people who weren't nice to their dogs. Ginger was a tease and a bully, and he had mean small eyes like a pig. Kathy's dad said what he needed was a good hard kick up the backside.

3

Kathy looked at the paper in Ginger's hand. 'What do you mean, it's worth money?' she demanded. 'It's just rubbish.'

Ginger spat his chewing-gum into the gutter and hitched up his dirty jeans. He smoothed out the wrapper and waved it in Kathy's face.

'Special offer, stupid,' he said grinning. 'All you do is collect the wrappers and send them off to Cooper's Candy Bars, Bristol. You get twenty pence for every ten wrappers you send.'

Kathy stared at him, her eyes round as teaplates. This could be just what she needed for that competition at school. The headmaster had announced it only the day before, and the prize was a brand-new bicycle. Kathy had dreamed all night of winning that bicycle for herself. Here was her chance.

Kathy grabbed the dangling paper from Ginger's fingers and shoved it quickly into her pocket.

'Thanks, Ginger,' she said, dodging out of his reach. And she ran off down the street and round the corner before he could stop her.

Kathy didn't see the sly grin on her cousin Ginger's face as he watched her

go. She was running so fast that she bumped straight into someone coming out of the sweet-shop door.

'Tim!' she said. 'You're just in time to help.'

Tim Barlow had black hair and blue eyes. He went to a different school, but he lived next door to Kathy and was her best friend.

'You should look where you're going,' he grumbled crossly. 'I nearly went under a bus. Fat lot of help I would be then.'

'Oh, shut up, Tim,' said Kathy impatiently. 'Come on. We've got to empty all the rubbish bins in Bunston before we go home for tea.'

Then, to Tim's astonishment, she picked up the litter bin outside the sweet shop and tipped all the rubbish into the street.

Chapter 2

It was dark when Kathy pushed open the back door and limped into the kitchen. She and Tim had walked miles round the streets of the town. They had emptied and sorted dozens of rubbish bins looking for the precious red and gold wrappers. And now Kathy was hungry and tired, and filthy from head to foot.

'What's for tea, Mam?' she said. 'I'm so hungry I could eat a giraffe.'

There was a smell of chips in the air. Kathy's mother was washing dishes, banging them noisily about to show that she wasn't pleased.

'You'll get no tea here at this time of night,' she snapped. 'And look at the state you're in. You look as if you spent the afternoon on the council rubbish tip.'

'That's a good idea,' said Kathy. 'I never thought of that.'

'Don't be cheeky to your mother,' said Kathy's dad, peering over the top of his computer magazine. But he got up and took a plate of sausages and chips out of the oven, winking at Kathy as he did so.

'Here, bonny lass,' he said. 'I kept it warm for you.'

After tea Kathy emptied her pockets and began to count the Cooper's Candy Bar wrappers on the kitchen table.

'Forty-nine, fifty, fifty-one,' she muttered to herself excitedly. 'I'll be a millionaire at this rate.'

'You can just get those dirty bits of paper off my clean table and get away to bed,' said Kathy's mother, screwing her mouth up as if she had swallowed a spoonful of nasty medicine.

'Aw, Mam. Just let me finish counting,' begged Kathy. 'Fifty-two, fifty-three, fifty-four! Wow! That's five twenty pences already. I wonder what colour my new bike will be.'

'What new bike?' said Kathy's dad, peering over his glasses. 'What are you talking about, lass?'

'The competition,' explained Kathy. 'At school. You know, to raise money for the new bike shed. That old wooden one's falling down.'

She shovelled the Cooper's Candy Bar

wrappers into a grocery bag. 'A thousand pounds we need, Mr Dobbs said. And whoever raises the most money by the end of term gets a brand-new bike.'

'I thought you were doing a sponsored swim,' said Kathy's dad.

'This is a better idea,' grinned Kathy.

'You get twenty pence for every ten wrappers you send away. I've got more than a pound's worth already.'

Kathy's mother moved grimly towards the table like a dentist with a drill.

'Bed,' she told Kathy firmly, and Kathy went. Her dad stuck his head round the bedroom door just as Kathy was climbing into bed.

'I'll spread the word round the factory,' he said. 'They sell hundreds of those things in the canteen.'

'Thanks, Dad,' murmured Kathy. And she fell asleep in no time, counting Cooper's Candy Bar wrappers instead of sheep.

Chapter 3

Next morning Kathy got up very early. She rummaged about in the garden shed until she found half a dozen empty cardboard boxes. Then she sat at the kitchen table writing labels for them in big letters with a felt-tip pen.

Kathy's mother came down yawning, her hair still in curlers.

'This is no time to be doing your homework,' she said sourly.

'It's not homework, Mam,' said Kathy. 'Honest.' And she held up one of the labels for her mother to see.

'PLEASE PUT YOUR COOPER'S

CANDY BAR WRAPPERS IN THIS BOX' it said, in bold black print.

Struggling along the street with the boxes piled up in her arms in front of her, Kathy bumped into three lamp-posts before she finally reached her first stop. She left the boxes outside and took only one of them with her into the sweet shop.

'Could you do me a favour, Mr Morgan?' she said, with a smile that showed all her dimples. And she explained what she wanted him to do.

By the time Kathy arrived at school she had only one box left. The others

were safely installed on the counters of all the sweet shops in town. Anyone who bought a Cooper's Candy Bar could put the wrapper straight into the box, and the shopkeepers had agreed to make sure they did so. Kathy felt so pleased with herself that she danced into school.

Mr Dobbs, the headmaster, was tall and thin and had long legs like a stork. He came out of his study just as Kathy was placing her last box in the main school hall. Kathy explained about the special offer.

'Twenty pence for every ten wrappers,

you say?' murmured Mr Dobbs thought-fully. 'The whole school should help with this. I'll mention it in Assembly.' And he stalked back into his study.

Kathy paid little attention to her lessons that day, and as soon as school was over she rushed round to her friend Tim's. Tim was waiting for her in the garden, his face and clothes covered in dirt, and tea-leaves and bits of bacon rind stuck in his hair. All around him on the lawn were little heaps of Cooper's Candy Bar wrappers.

'Look what I've got!' Tim said. 'I've been crawling about the council tip.'

'I was going to suggest that,' said Kathy. 'You look like something the dog dragged off the compost heap. How many did you get?'

'About a hundred,' said Tim jubilantly. 'But that's not the best bit.' He began to hop up and down on the grass with excitement. Bits of potato peel fell off him to the ground.

'You know my dad works for Radio Newcastle, don't you?' he said. 'Well . . . you'll never guess!'

'What, Tim? What?' cried Kathy,

giving her friend a push that sent him tumbling among the wrappers.

Tim sat up, grinning.

'He's getting you on the Children's Show,' he said. 'You're going to be on the radio, Kathy Sharpe!'

Chapter 4

Kathy's legs felt like boiled spaghetti and her mouth was dry. She cleared her throat for the hundredth time and glanced nervously at Mike James, the Children's Show interviewer.

A red light went on and Mike nodded at Kathy. It was time.

'Good afternoon, kids,' Mike said breezily into the microphone. 'This is your pal Mike James with another hour of jokes, stories and music for the young

at heart. And in today's Secret Ambition spot we have a little lady who is helping her school to raise a thousand pounds. Tell us about it, Kathy.'

Kathy took a deep breath and spoke into the microphone in front of her. And to her surprise she suddenly found that she wasn't nervous at all. She told the story about the competition, and saving the Cooper's Candy Bar wrappers, and begged all the children who were listening to save them, too.

'And you can send all of those candy bar wrappers to Kathy at twenty-seven, Seymour Street, Bunston,' Mike put in,

when Kathy paused for breath. 'Or you can take them to the Grove Road Junior School. How about it, kids? Are you going to help Kathy Sharpe to achieve her Secret Ambition?' And he gave Kathy a thumbs-up signal.

Outside in the corridor Kathy's dad squeezed her hand. 'You were great, bonny lass,' he said. 'I was so proud of you I nearly burst. Wasn't she great, Mam?'

Kathy's mother sniffed as if there was a bad smell under her nose.

'I suppose so,' she said. 'But the house is full already. I don't know where we'll put any more.'

The Cooper's Candy Bar wrappers had been pouring in from all directions. Several other schools had decided to help, and three big factory canteens, as well as sweet shops in nearby towns. Kathy's bedroom was so full of wrappers

that she could hardly get into bed. The living room was stacked to the ceiling with boxes, and they had to climb over more boxes to reach the kitchen sink. Kathy couldn't even guess how much they were all worth.

When Kathy and her parents got home from the studio they couldn't get the car into the drive. More sackfuls of wrappers had been delivered while they were out, and Tim was sitting on the front lawn counting feverishly.

'There must be about a million!' he shouted when he saw Kathy.

Kathy's mother folded her arms and scowled. 'I'm not putting up with this any longer,' she said grimly. 'You'll have to keep them somewhere else.' She squeezed her way through the piles of boxes to the front door.

Kathy looked helplessly at her dad.

'Don't worry, pet,' he said. 'I'll borrow the firm's van on Saturday. I'm sure Mr Dobbs will let you keep the wrappers at school.'

And off he went to telephone the headmaster.

Chapter 5

By the time Saturday came nobody in Kathy's house could move for Cooper's Candy Bar wrappers. Sackful upon sackful had arrived after the radio show, and every room was now piled up from floor to ceiling. Even the bathroom was crammed full, and Kathy hadn't had a bath for almost a week.

Cooper's Candy Bar wrappers filled the garden, packed in plastic binbags to keep them dry, and more bags marched down the drive towards the street, like fat black soldiers.

There were thousands more wrappers at school. Kathy's broadcast had been repeated on other radio stations, and parcels had poured in from all over the country. Every available space was crammed with Cooper's Candy Bar wrappers, and the headmaster could hardly get into his study.

Kathy and Tim had given up counting them. There were just too many. But

Kathy knew that at twenty pence for every ten wrappers there would certainly be enough for a new bike shed. There were probably enough for a whole new school.

The old bike shed in the school grounds hadn't been used for some time. The wooden timbers were weak and rotten, and the building had been declared unsafe. There was plenty of room to store the Cooper's Candy Bar wrappers, however, and Mr Dobbs had even agreed to give up his Saturday golf in order to help.

Moving all those wrappers took a long time. Tim and Mr Dobbs worked hard all morning, lugging sacks and boxes from the school building across the playing field to the shed, while Kathy and her dad drove backwards and forwards from home to school in the firm's van. When the very last sackful was finally pushed into the shed, and the creaky old door fastened shut, Tim and

Kathy flung themselves down on the grass. Mr Dobbs wiped his face on his hanky.

'I wish I'd never heard of Cooper's Candy Bar wrappers,' groaned Tim.

'I'm never going to eat another one as long as I live,' muttered Kathy.

Kathy's dad prodded them with his toe.

'Come on, kids,' he said. 'I'll buy us all some fish and chips for lunch.'

Chapter 6

Kathy spent the rest of the weekend dreaming about her new bike, and on Monday morning she climbed over the latest delivery of wrappers and hurried off to **school**. The blow fell as soon as sh**e got there.**

Kathy's teacher, Miss Potter, had a **crumpled face t**hat looked as if it needed ir**oning. She h**ad a red nose and red eyes and **she sniffe**d all the time because of her hay **fever**. Kathy had seen her wiping her nose **on** her sleeve when she thought no-one was looking.

Miss Potter was waiting for Kathy at the classroom door.

'Mr Dobbs wants to see you, Kathy Sharpe,' she said ominously. The other children stared curiously, and Kathy put out her tongue before setting off along the corridor.

Mr Dobbs was striding angrily about his office when Kathy tapped and pushed open the door.

'I've had a phone call this morning,' he snapped, glaring at her. 'From Cooper's Candy Bars of Bristol. They've heard all about your radio appeal.'

Kathy gazed at a hole in the carpet while the headmaster stamped about and kicked a box of Cooper's Candy Bar wrappers from one end of the room to the other. She knew something awful was about to happen.

'COOPER'S CANDY BARS DON'T KNOW ANYTHING ABOUT IT!'

shouted Mr Dobbs suddenly, banging his fist down on the desk. 'You have been wasting your time. AND everybody else's! Do you understand what I'm saying, child? THERE IS NO SPECIAL OFFER!'

Kathy's mouth fell open. She stared at the headmaster, unable to believe her ears.

'But . . . there must be!' she stammered at last. 'My cousin Ginger said . . .'

'Your cousin Ginger has been mistaken,' glowered Mr Dobbs. 'Or he has deliberately misled you. A joke, I suppose.'

Kathy knew which was more likely. She'd murder that rotten Ginger when she got her hands on him.

'I suggest you make sure of your facts, next time,' hissed the headmaster, almost spitting in his rage. 'And I don't care how you do it , but just get rid of them all, do you hear ? You may take the day off

school to do it, but I want every chocolate wrapper off these premises by four
o'clock. You can start with this lot!'

Mr Dobbs shoved the box of wrappers
into Kathy's arms with such force that
she almost fell over.

'NOW GET OUT OF MY SIGHT!'
he shouted.

Kathy ran for her life.

Chapter 7

Kathy let herself into the house. Her mother and father were at work, Tim was at school, and there was nobody to help her. How could she get rid of those chocolate wrappers all by herself? It was impossible.

A tear slid down Kathy's face and she wiped it away with her hand. There'd be no new bike after all. What a slob that Ginger was.

Kathy pulled herself together. There must be something she could do. Then her eyes widened, and she stared at the table by her dad's chair, where he kept his favourite pipe and his box of matches.

Matches! She grabbed the box and raced back to school.

Everybody was still in class and the grounds were deserted. Kathy dragged the bike shed door open and began to heave sacks and boxes of Cooper's Candy Bar wrappers one by one into the middle of the school field. She was so desperate, she didn't think of the danger. She knew there was no other way.

Kathy struck a match and put it to a little heap of spilled wrappers. The waxed paper caught fire easily, and in no time at all the flames spread. Soon all the wrappers were blazing away like a Guy Fawkes bonfire.

A big lump came into Kathy's throat as she watched her hard work go up in flames. There were shouts as people ran out of the school towards the field.

A sudden gust of wind sprang up and blew bits of burning paper around the field and up against the bike-shed door. The dry old timbers started to smoulder. Before Kathy could do anything except gape in horror, flames began to creep up the shed walls and clouds of black smoke poured into the sky.

Kathy turned and fled.

Chapter 8

A special meeting had been announced and the whole school waited in the hall. The headmaster cleared his throat and gazed down at them from the platform. It was so quiet you could have heard a feather fall.

'Will Kathleen Sharpe come up here, please,' he called.

Everybody knew that the bike-shed fire had been Kathy's fault. They nudged one another and whispered as she made her way to the front.

Kathy had already been questioned by the police and a man from the insurance company, and she had thought that the worst was over. But now Mr Dobbs was going to tell her off in front of the whole school. Kathy trembled as she stood facing them all.

'You all know that Kathy has been in serious trouble,' began Mr Dobbs, and his voice sounded kind. 'The police and the insurance company, however, are quite satisfied that the fire was an accident.'

Mr Dobbs shuffled some papers in his

hand. 'It now appears that the old bicycle shed was insured,' he said. 'This means that the insurance company will pay for a new one to be built, since it seems clear that no deliberate attempt to burn it was involved.'

The headmaster waved one of his bits of paper in the air.

'I have here,' he announced grandly, 'a cheque for the sum of ONE THOUSAND POUNDS!'

Kathy felt dizzy as if she were about to faint. The whole school buzzed with excitement. The commotion grew louder

as Mr Hoppings, the games teacher, came in wheeling a shining new yellow bicycle.

Mr Dobbs held up his hand. 'Kathy's actions have been foolish and dangerous,' he said gently, 'but her intentions were always good. And as a result we have gained the new shed that we needed so badly. I have therefore no hesitation in announcing the winner of the competition. Kathy Sharpe!' And everybody cheered and yelled and stamped their feet.

Kathy had never been so happy in her life. She sang at the top of her voice as she rode home on her new yellow bike, waving proudly at everyone she knew. And one of the first people she saw was her cousin Ginger.

Ginger's mouth dropped open in astonishment when he saw the new bicycle. Kathy gave him a cheery wave.

'That was a great idea, collecting those

Cooper's Candy Bar wrappers,' she shouted. 'Look what I got with them!'

Ginger looked first baffled, then furious. Kathy swerved the bike towards him and ran over his foot.

'Ow!' yelled Ginger, hopping up and down. And he said a very rude word.

Kathy didn't care. She rode happily homewards, looking forward to fried chicken for supper.

First published in Great Britain in 1986 by
Marilyn Malin Books in association with André Deutsch Ltd.
105 Great Russell Street, London WC1B 3LJ

Conceived, designed and produced by Belitha Press Ltd.
2 Beresford Terrace, London N5 2DH
Copyright in this format © Belitha Press 1986
Text copyright © Sheila Lavelle 1986
Illustrations copyright © Glenys Ambrus 1986
Series design by Peter Wingham

10 9 8 7 6 5 4 3 2 1

ISBN 0 233 97948 4

Printed in Spain.

B76